CAMINAR

CAMINAR

SKILA BROWN

CANDLEWICK PRESS

Copyright © 2014 by Skila Brown

First edition 2014

Library of Congress Catalog Card Number 2013946611
ISBN 978-0-7636-6516-6

13 14 15 16 17 18 BVG 10 9 8 7 6 5 4 3 2 1

Printed in Berryville, VA, U.S.A.

This book was typeset in Adobe Caslon Pro.

Candlewick Press
99 Dover Street
Somerville, Massachusetts 02144

visit us at www.candlewick.com

In memory of the

more than 200,000 people

who were killed or disappeared in Guatemala

between 1960 and 1996.

May they always be remembered.

A Note to the Reader

In 1954, the democratically elected government of Guatemala was overthrown by a group of military men who were unhappy with the way the government had been passing laws to help poor farmers in rural communities. Forty horrible years followed, in which the people of Guatemala tried to resist, organize, and bring about change, all while the Guatemalan army did everything they could to discourage the "rebels" or "guerillas," as they called the organizers. The army went into the mountains of rural Guatemala, where they tried to prevent villagers from joining the rebels.

Many lives were lost. And many more were never the same.

Chopán, Guatemala, 1981

Where I'm From

Our mountain stood tall,
like the finger that points.

Our corn plants grew in fields,
thick and wide as a thumb.

Our village sat in the folded-between,
in that spot where you pinch something sacred,

to keep it still.

Our mountain stood guard at our backs.
We slept at night in its bed.

Ah Xochil

Mama called me
Ah Xochil:
round face of an

                  Owl

quiet moon face
stretched so wide
all filled up with

                  Eyes

head that swiveled
side to side
moving just to

                  See

silent when the
day birds sang
I sat, away from

                  All

Not Yet

I was strong enough
to break the wood into small pieces and feed
our fire. I kept our stove top warm.
>   But Mama would not send me out to cut a tree. "Not yet,"
>   she said, and put away the blade.

I was old enough
to feed the chickens, gather eggs
by myself. I watched out for them all.
>   But Mama would not let me wring their necks. "Not yet,"
>   she said, and wiped her brow, feathers stuck to her arm with blood.

Soccer

I did not have to be big—just strong
enough to make a wall
with my body,
keep everyone   away
from the ball at my feet.

Then I could move,
    tap it   from one foot   to the next,
go down the field   and never lose
the ball.

I could move the ball
safely, closer to the goal,
close enough to score,
but I was too afraid
it would be   taken
before it reached the goal.
So I passed
      instead. Even though Mateo's shot
                  didn't make it, I sighed with relief.
                        Because my pass did.

Almost Dark

When I felt my eyes start to pinch,
trying to see the ball, I knew
Mama wanted me home.
      "I have to go. *Lo siento, amigos.*"
Without me, the teams were
unbalanced, so I heard my friends complain:

                "Don't go!"
                "Cinco minutos más."
                "Not now!"
                "Why?"

Mateo answered before I could.   "Leave Carlos
                  alone. It is his bedtime.
                  You know he is afraid
                  of the dark."

Roberto tried to catch
my eye, but I looked away.

My cheeks
   burned. My neck
   itched. I tucked my chin down
   into my chest, my shoulders pointed
   toward my feet, which pointed to home.

Roberto

Roberto had a brother, Davíd,
who was old enough to
>   pick the cherry coffee fruits,
>   hold a girl's hand on his way to church,
>   smoke a cigarette behind the *tienda,*
and old enough to
>   have the military knock on his door
>   with signing papers.

Roberto had a father, Manuel,
who was drunk enough to
>   yell
>   at the officers who
>   knocked on his door,
>   hunting for
>   soldier sons.

   And then,
   after that,

Roberto and his mother lit
>   a candle in the church
>   for the son,
>   the soldier son,
>   Davíd, now with a gun.

Roberto and his mother lit
>   a candle in the church
>   for the father,
>   Roberto's father,
>   Manuel, who was gone.

Soldiers Set Up Camp

That year before the rains began, they came
in jeeps, with tents for sleep,
set up camp outside our village.

I said, "There are so many
of them. How will they all fit inside those tents?"
    Tía Rosa said, "They brought more
    bullets than corn."
        Roberto's mother said, "They have no
        right to be here. We have done nothing
        wrong."
            Santiago said, "They are not here
            for us. Their prey is in the jungle.
            They are hunters."
                Mama said, "They are boys.
                Men, far away from home. With nothing good
                to eat."

                She would not let me take
                the bread she sent
                to them, did not want me to get   close.

Close

One night, three of them
came to our soccer field, watched
a bit, then joined in.

They were not that bad.

When the game was over, they passed out
sodas, asked if anyone wanted a job.
The big one, with a laugh
that wheezed like a teasing
balloon, said,
        "Just bring me the names
        of any Communists you know. All we want
        are names."

I did not know what a Communist was, never
heard that word before said in our village, did not know
what it meant, did not understand.

But the 400 *quetzales* they offered?
        Enough to feed a person
            for a month, or buy
                a radio in San Fernando.

I looked at the faces of my
friends and knew
that was something we all understood.

The Army

The soldiers stayed for days,
at the foot of our mountain.
They ate tortillas, played soccer, listened to music,
just like us. But
they were always searching, always
watching, always serious,
warning us about guerillas. Warning
us about those rebel Communists. Warning us
to keep them away.

They even let a few boys shoot their guns.
We were not scared.
                              But then,
the day before the army broke up camp and left,
some women who were washing clothes came
running back to town   screaming

          Roberto and I walked
          toward the water to see what made them run.

                    It was a man
                                   Juan Choc Túc
               dangling
                              from a tree
          a sign was hung
          from the rope around
          his neck: COMMUNIST.

                              I heard the soldiers, packing
                              up their things, laughing.
                              "Para que escarmienten."
                              "They will learn a lesson."

I watched some men from my village come cut
the rope, lower his body

11

stiff
carry it back to town.

I heard them talking about
      Juan Choc Túc.
They were not calling him a Communist, instead
they spoke of land
he owned, land others wanted, land
no one could afford, unless
they earned a few *quetzales*
selling names
to the army.

Later That Night

The soldiers called us all
into the middle of the village. I could
still see that stiff body in my mind, and so I did not want to go.
Mama said, "Come, *mijo*. It is best if we just see what it is
they want." But all they wanted was a chance
to stand high on the steps,
grip their guns tight to their chests,
watch us all wait to hear their words.

They were passing out food,
sodas, just a few things they did not want
to bother hauling away the next day.
Even though we were all forced to come,
there were not enough sweets to go around.

        The big one, with the balloon laugh, said, "Remember,
            there are traitors in this village, people
            who are spies for the rebels,
            snakes who want to carry
        harm into Chopán. When we come back, we will pay
            money for these names, reward those
            who do their part to keep this village safe
              from the terrorists
            who want to tear it all apart."

                He was not
          laughing his wheezy laugh.

He reminded us there was a war
going on. They were working hard to find and kill
the enemy, keep us safe.
     "Remember," he said. "These men are rebels,
     stupid smelly pigs," he spat. "They are guerillas,

ugly clumsy things," he spat. "They are Communists who
will come, steal your food, hurt your women, take
your children. They cannot be trusted.

Offer them no help.

You must defend your village."

I wondered how many soldiers these rebels must have killed,
to make the army hate them so.

On the Way Home

The army said the Communists were bad,
evil, wanting to take away
the land that people owned. I did not know anyone
who owned any land,
so I was not worried.
Santiago, on his way to his stool by the corn, said, "Land
does not belong to anyone."

The Next Morning

We watched them leave, shaking
their heads from side to side,
jeeps bouncing on the road,
dust flying up behind.

Some people worried,
        didn't want them to go, felt unsafe.
Some people sighed,
        didn't want them to stay, felt unsafe.

I was not sure why they were leaving,
without the rebels they said they came to find.

        Mateo's brother said, "We must be ready to fight
        the rebels."
Roberto's mother said, "It is the army
we should fight, battle them if they come again."

        Santiago said, "It is not
        our war."

Roberto was looking down,
not making a sound.

        Mateo was nodding his head up and down,
        up and down. "It is up to
        us to keep our village safe."
        He turned to Roberto then, frowned,
        said, "It is time
        to be a man."

Roberto said
nothing.   I nodded, said, "Keep our village safe."

The oldest of Flora's brothers
laughed
and said, "The troubles
of our nation — solved
by a bunch of schoolboys."

Flora

Flora
    lived   in my village
    climbed trees   with me   when her father
        wasn't looking
      showed me the spot
        in her grandmother's garden where she buried
        a puppy one year

Flora
    lived   with her family
    mother, father, three sisters, four brothers, two grandmothers,
    and an uncle   all
    under the same roof
    always loud   always busy   never enough   food

Sometimes
    when Mama and I finished our meal
      at the table with two chairs,
      I would wrap some beans into a tortilla,
      tuck it into my pocket,
      walk to Flora's house, watch her
      eat on the steps,
        lick her fingers,
          laugh at me as I
            tried to pluck a feather
              from Señor Pancho, the rooster,
                  her fingers wrapped around the edge
                    of the tortilla, her teeth peeking out,
                  her mouth in a smile.

Healer

Flora's grandmother had a garden,
behind their house, full of plants growing
    as food and full of plants growing
    to heal. But the most important
plants she gathered from the jungle,
teaching Flora to look for
    leaves pointed, berries yellow, roots moist.
Flora and her sisters and their mother would
    chop and wash, mash and boil,
while her grandmother
    looked on, looked over,
as they made the healing paste, making sure
they got each mixture just right, making sure
there would always be a healer in that house,
    mending, helping, listening
to the pains of the whole town.

In the Fields

The day after the soldiers left, I did not
go to school, I went to work instead
with Mateo and his uncles, in the coffee fields,
where berries fat and red waited
inside the bushes
to be picked.
I ran my fingers down the stem,
pulled them toward me with a crackle,
my hands were fast,
squeezing life from each bush,
squeezing out the promise of tomorrow,
red sweet hope,
ready to be plucked,
red juicy life,
ready to fill the basket at my waist,

my hands moved fast down each stem,
crackle
c r a c k l e
crackle,
like climbing a rope except I was not
going anywhere.

Being a Man

When my work was done, I took the long path
home, looking for Flora, to show her the money
I earned for a day of being a man.
I could not find her near the corn, where
Santiago was sitting, keeping
away hungry animals. I did find
      Mama there, looking for me.

      "¿Carlos, *dónde andabas?* Where have you been? Luisa tells me
      you did not go to school?"

"School is for children, Mama. Today,
I am a man." I dug
into my pocket, pulled out
money from inside, put each
centavo in her hand.

      Mama shut her eyes
      tight, shut her mouth
      tight, shut her fist around the money tight,
      tight, tight.
      "You are too young,
      mijo, to work in fields all day."

I moved my eyes to Santiago's stool, where he
sat, saying nothing.

"I am old enough," I said.

      Mama sighed, shook her head, told me to come home
      soon, then walked away.

I smiled, because she kept
the money in her hands, money
to buy food, money that I earned myself.

Nahuales

Santiago's voice called out to me,
     worn and warm and old,
"I was your age when I stepped away
from Child,   stepped into Man."

I looked over at him then.
     He took his cane and pointed
     up the mountainside.
     "In the woods,
     I met my *nahual,*
     became a man."

I looked up to the trees,
away from his eyes. I did not want to tell him
no one believes anymore
in *nahuales,*
spirit animals who guide us in life, keep us
safe.   I walked away.
         But I wondered
           which animal
             he saw.

Santiago Luc

Santiago Luc
                was the oldest
man I knew, older than
Flora's *abuela* who had lived
seventy-six years, older than *el tío de* Mateo who turned
eighty that June, older than my *abuela,* who—for ninety years—
had lived at the top of the mountain, in the tiniest
village, that I had made the climb to see
only once.

Mateo said Santiago Luc was older
than the trees, older
than the mountain, older
than dirt.

Santiago Luc said he did not know
how many years he had walked the land, but he remembered
a time when everyone
        wore the colors of our village, the colors that only a few
        still wove into cloth so bright,
a time when no one
        had to walk for days to find
        a plot of land to plant some food,
a time when there were no soldiers
        driving up in jeeps, holding
            meetings, making
                laws, scattering
                    bullets into the trees,
                        hunting guerillas.

Guerilla Rain

They came
in rain,
the end
of wet
season, when
rain was
no longer
welcome.

      Yet
it beat
our roof,
turned floor
to mud,
washed off
the army
camp.
      Guerillas.

They came
in rain.
We huddled
inside, waited
for earth
to stop
its   slide.

They came,
sacks   empty
bellies   empty
guns   full.

      Rebels.

They marched
right through
our town,
made their
way into
the jungle.

And when
the last
of them
had been
sucked in
by thick
green arms,

the rain
stopped.

What My Eyes Saw from the Window

They were not aiming
for our village.
They just cut through.

They were not beaten down
by rain, or mud, or roads that would not stay.

They were not loading up their arms
with what we had inside.

Instead they raised
their hands, waved,
then shot us smiles.

What Roberto Said

"They are wearing clothes like soldiers, look
exactly like the army, no signs that say Communist
strapped on their backs at all.

"They did not
stop to hurt us, did not
prick our village, did not
take   anything   at all."

What Mama Said

"They will
be back."

Mama Was Right

Two mornings passed after they climbed
into the mouth of the jungle.
           I did not think
            they would come back.

I was standing
behind the *tienda* with Roberto,
           drinking a Pepsi,
           when they came:

        two men
with hats that matched
the colors of the trees,
        a woman
with boots
higher than her knees,
        and a boy,
a boy.

Not yet
as tall
as me.

He Had a Gun

A rifle rattled
on his shoulder,

his thumb tucked
under the strap,

a shadow where
a mustache planned to grow, above his lip.

He tapped his fingers
on the bullets around his waist

as he winked
at some girls.

Roberto dropped his Pepsi,
ducked inside.

My feet stuck
right to the ground.

I did not move.
Except my eyes.

They Walked

They walked
down the hill
and into the

village.

We froze
so still
the whole

Tortillas

Everyone found
something to do inside.

Everyone except Mama.

She sat on her stool by the fire.
Her hands were doing
what they always did:

Pinching the dough
Squeeze   Twist
          Squeeze
                    Twist
Dance of the wrist.
          CLAP CLAP CLAP

The village silent
except for her hands.
          CLAP CLAP CLAP

Four guerillas walked right up to her.
          CLAP CLAP CLAP CLAP
          CLAP CLAP CLAP
          CLAP CLAP
          CLAP

Mama and the Communists

Nod

               Nod

Nod

               How are you?

Fine, thank you.

               Beautiful day.

               Tortillas?

Nod

               Nod

Nod

               How much to pay?

Take what you need.

Before They Left

The one who did all the
talking, the one with the red
bandanna around his neck, thanked
my mother
for the tortillas, then asked her about
the *tzut* in her hair.
> It was the yellow one, the one with birds
> of all colors puffed out with woven thread like they were sitting
> on her head,   the same one made when
> she was a girl, the same one she wore every day and no one ever
> thought to talk about.

"Qué bonita," he said. "How beautiful."

She smiled.   They left.

After They Left

"They are rebels."

"They have
guns."   "Blood on their hands."

"They march ahead of
        trouble."   "You'll see."
"Best if they
                move on."

                    "They did us no
harm."   "Blood."

"It's not safe."

                    "Remember Juan Choc Túc?"
"¡Mi Manuel!"
        "Pobrecito."
                "We must protect our village."   "They have
guns."   *"Dios mío."*
                "¡Blood!"

                    "We want no part."

Mama: "Everyone has to eat."

Three Days

Three days passed
since the rebels came and went.
Enough time for them to be far
up in the jungle, buried
in the trees.

For Three Whole Days

People in our village whispered,
argued,
wondered what to do.

"The rebels will return, we must
be prepared."   "The army!"
          "The army will come
          back and smell guerilla in the air."   "They want
     names."   *"Dios mío."*
"We must tell them where they went."   "You!"
                              "I saw you talk to them."
                                        "Tell them
     nothing."   "I am not
                         a Communist!"

                                        I stayed away
                               from the edge of trees,
                           stayed close to home, one
                                 eye out the window,
                            watching,   waiting.

What the Village Decided

I was sitting on the front doorstep,
with Roberto and Mateo, when
Angel Choc Có came to tell Mama, "Run.
Our village is not safe. If the rebels
or the army
return to Chopán,
we should all   run,
  go to the
        trees, hide. Run."

She wiped her hands on her apron,
nodded, looked first up
at the mountain and then down
at me, as Angel left to deliver
the message to someone else.

                Mateo stood up,
                said, "A man
                does not run.
                I will stay
                and defend our village, protect
                everyone in Chopán."

                Roberto said
                nothing.

                I nodded,
                stood up next to Mateo, said, "We
                will not run.
                We must fight for Chopán."

"Mateo, Roberto, go home now," Mama said.
She looked at me with narrow eyes.
"You. Come inside so we can talk."

I heard Mateo
as I closed the door, "Carlos always does
what he is told."

In the Doorway with Mama

She did not
sit down, did not
take more than two steps. Just
pointed her finger right to me,
"You
will
run."

"Mama, I—"

"No.
Carlos, I do not want to hear
a word.
Listen to me. You
will run. When you hear
the first sign of trouble,
you will go.

We will meet in the mountains,
go as deep as you can.
Do not slow down, do not
look back.

You will do this because
boys in this village
do as they are told, do just
what the elders say."

"I will wait for you."

"You will find me,"
she said.
"Maybe not right away."

She took my chin in her
hand, pulled my eyes
up to hers.
"But, Carlos,
you will
find me."

The Next Day

Mama
left the house of Tía Rosa
after the baby
took her first breath.

Mama
came back down to our house,
her apron wet,
her face flushed and damp,
tired from a night without sleep,
a night of bringing a baby
into this world.

Mama
smiled, asked me
to gather mushrooms
while she went to rest her eyes.
"Wake me when you get back
so I can make the soup."

The thought
of going into the jungle
made my heart, my eyes blink and flap like a baby
bird, pushed
off the branch for the very first time.

But I only said,
"Sí, Mama,"
picked up the marbles I was shooting,
put them into my pocket,
took a bag from the nail on the side of the shed,
turned toward the mountain.

"Carlos."

                I stopped.

"Another sweater."

                I groaned. I had my T-shirt, my jacket. I
                was warm enough.
"It is warmer here than
there." Her lips pointed up
to the trees and the climb.

                I stomped inside, grabbed
                the first one I felt on the hook,
                stomped back, past
    Mama.

She reached out her hand to ruffle
my hair but
                I was already gone.

To the Mountain

The house of Tía Rosa was still,
quiet when I walked by, pulling me like a string to
peek into the window, see
    if my new cousin was awake.
    But I did not. Instead
    I walked to the edge of the village,
    passed the *tienda,* the church, the lake that waits
    underneath and catches the water that falls
    down the side of the
mountain. I took off my
    shoes, waded through
    to the cornfield.
    Santiago's stool—empty. Daytime does not need
guards to keep the *maíz* safe from hungry
    animals. In the day, it was the place of play for all
children:
    rows to run down,
    stalks so high a child can
hide and not be seen
    by adults who call. I walked
    past and saw
    Flora, her younger sister,
    wrapped to her back, tugging
    her hair. She
    waved.
    "¡Carlos, *vení aquí!*"
    But I kept walking,
    too tall to hide,
safe among the stalks, anymore.

Sounds

I walked closer to the trees,
heard the sound of birds
    get louder, sound of leaves
      catching the wind
        get louder, sound of the mountain getting
          louder and louder.

        Behind me
        the laughter from the
        cornfield, the noises from the
      village, the rumble
    of trucks
    approaching,

all disappeared.

Mama Was Making Soup

Mama was making soup.
She sent me to gather mushrooms.
Santiago taught me which ones are
sacred,   which ones are
bitter,   which ones are
sweet,   which ones cause
death.   So I went.
Mama was making soup.
Sopa de hongos.
So I left.   I went
into the jungle. Deep.
Mama was making soup.

I could not see the village.
And it could not see me.

Why I Dropped the Mushrooms

                    pop
            pop
            pop pop pop pop
pop   pop   pop
            pop   pop

            it sounded like
            cohetes
            on a saint's day—
            fireworks—

                except for the

                                        screams

Blind

I did not see

       blades
       spinning in the sky
I did not see   bullets
          raining
          down
I did not see

                 screams
           prayers
         soldiers yelling
I did not see

                   feet running
                   shots
              shots
          shots
     screams

I did not see

         I stood there, still
         as a tree, deep

         in the woods,

               eyes closed,

               ears left open

I Climbed a Tree

in out in
out in out in
out in out in out
in out in out in out in
out in *my breath was fast*
step pull step pull step pull step
pull step pull step pull step pull
step pull *I climbed a tree*

arms squeezed
tree swayed

eyes closed

I

disappeared

Even When

I stayed in my tree
even when

their machetes sliced
the edges of the jungle,
their voices pricked
the loud whir of Nothing
that roared in my ears.

I stayed in my tree
even when

the pops of their rifles,
laughter of the soldiers,
screams of my neighbors all
    died down.

I stayed in my tree
even when

my tree caught the whisper
blowing from tree to tree, a message
wave, turning leaves right side up
brighter green,
a message that said:
                They're gone.

Laughter

Above the laughs so round and plain
they could have come from any
mouth,   I had heard

                    the wheeze.

Who?

I would have stayed
a branch, never moving again,
except

> *Who?*

Through eyes shut tight and ears turned
off, I heard it:
> *uu uuu*

My eyes
unclenched.

> *Who?*

Darkness.
> *uu uuu*

Night everywhere.

> *Who?*

My eyes
could not see.
> *uu uuu*

I turned my neck,
stiff neck,

> *Who?*

My eyes landed on   Eyes
        uu uuu
rounder than mine.
Big black circles

                    Who?

full of nothing but
Calm.
        uu uuu
El tecolote.

                    Who?

The owl.

Stare

we

both

s t a r e d

eyes

big

and

r o u n d

and

did

not

make

a

s o u n d

His Eyes

His eyes said
nothing,   asked
nothing,   held
nothing,   but
mine.

My lungs

slowed.

My arms

unclenched.

My heart:

se durmió.

I stared into his eyes

until I fell

asleep.

asleep

I stand on the edge
of the branch and dive
stretch my arms out wide
enough to glide

fly

swim through the air over the trees
to see
the lake below
still, quiet,
red

I see
the people of my village on the bank, the water's edge,
no one speaking,
just walking,
walking down
into a trench, wide and deep,
one at a time, walking
down, lying flat,
falling asleep,

they are not
smiling and yet no one seems
anything but calm

I see
Tía Rosa with a bundle in her arms
I try to go in closer, get
close enough to see
but the wind picks up again,
Tía Rosa enters the trench,
points behind her, so I
fly on

I see Roberto and Mateo, Santiago
holds his cane, uses it to point
behind him

I see
Flora

she looks at me with eyes so
kind, does not move her mouth to form
any words but I feel her speak to me
Go.
I do not want to leave
her face but she moves me with her eyes
points behind
I see
yellow
cloth, birds perched
on blackest hair—

Mama

is walking
closer to the trench, silent
with the others and I feel a tug
start to close my arms up to my chest
let myself
fall to the ground
but the wind won't let me,
keeps me in the air, keeps me
away from Chopán
I look into her face

it says
Go.

I feel her push me
with her mind, push me to look behind
I try to stop the force that keeps
me in the air, try to follow
her but I am no match for
the wind
and I feel her move it with her mind

You will find me.

Behind her is our mountain.

The wind
carries me there.

The Next Morning

The owl was

        gone.

The branch was

        empty.

Birds of

        day, before

me flew.

        Every one

of them

safe,

home.

Mariposas

I looked, pointed
   my eyes toward the village, toward
      Chopán. Looked through
         trees to see. Something
           moved. Something
               fell. A limb.

              CRASH.

              And then — the sky
                 was filled
                    with blue,   butterflies,
                tiny blues
            that fluttered and flew,
          past my tree,
        over my head, above
       the forest,
      into the sky.
    I blinked
    and saw
   the last one
was yellow.

Back on the Ground

I did not want to climb down, but I did,
                    one foot under the other.

I did not want to look around, but I did,
                trees, sun — just a   day.

I did not want to leave that spot, but I did,
                 tiptoeing to the edge of the wood.

I did not want to leave my village, but
   the wind pushed my legs,
      pushed them up the mountain, kept
    me from walking down,
         kept me safe.

I Walked

My legs brushed

against the bush,

swish swash

swish.

I walked.

My tracks

cracked

the sticks.

Forest sounds

all around

but on the ground

the sound

of Me

grew. Echoed.

I heard a path I could not see.

it did not happen
it did not happen
did not happen
did not happen
not happen
not happen
not
not

not
no

Argument with a Boy

                         I walked.

Is she alive?

                                        Yes.   Yes.
                         I walked.

                                        Yes. She promised
                                                to run.

                         I walked.

How will I find her?

                         I walked.

                                        I will look.

                         I walked.

Should I go back?
What if she is there?
What if?

                         I walked.

                                        She ran. She is
                                        here. She is safe.

                         I walked.

Everyone else?

                         I walked.

What about everyone else?

                         I walked.

                                        Mama told me to run.

                         I walked.

Only boys run.

                         I walked.

"Carlos always does what he is told."
What would Mateo do?

                         I walked.

He would go back.

                         I walked.

                                        I will find Mama. She
                                        will know what to do.

                         I walked.

Now who is the child?

64

Tired

I was so tired,
empty of fuel,
my legs limp
and weak.

Muscles hot
and numb,
body   heavy   empty   weak and I was
so tired

        tears ran
            down my face

            tears

                    ran
                        I stopped

                    i was so   tired

When I Stopped

I found a tree
that looked softer than most,
stronger than me.

I climbed a little — just enough
to put air between
the earth and me

but close enough that
earth would be
only a short fall away.

I climbed up,
tucked in my feet
underneath

my legs. But my feet
kept rocking
back and forth,

pinching open, pinching shut. My feet
walked still
in my sleep.

When I Woke Up

I took my arms away
from the tree. They burned

stiff and did not believe my brain, which
told them they could stop their clinging

to a tree that was no longer there,
nothing left to grip but air.

My arms did not care,
did not seem to hear.

So I opened my mouth to tell them Let Go,
but when I stretched my lips they cracked.

I opened my mouth and tasted
the air, and it tasted so new,

I realized my mouth had been
closed for a long time.

I sucked in a breath and pushed it out
with a whisper.
                                        "Let Go."

My voice crumbled
like wood after a fire,

so I licked my lips.
I tasted blood.

Water

How long since I had
eaten? I didn't want to
count back the past to see.

I knew I needed
water. My tongue was thick and had shut my jaws
and made the trees spin and I needed to get

water. Outside the forest where the trees thin,
there is sun.
There is water,

a stream that flows down
into my village
all the way from

Patrichál, the village
at the mountain's top, the village where
my grandmother lived.

I Drank from the Stream

Water rushing
 down the mountain
  in a hurry
   because it thought

   it was needed
    at the bottom
     of the mountain
      where people wait:

   by the big rocks,
    laundry stretched out,
     women laughing—
      they've had their drinks.

    Crops are thirsty,
     children dirty,
      village needs it,
       water can't wait.

        Buckets to fill,
                soups to make,
                        mouths to kiss,

                                          but

         there was just mine.
        What would the water find?

Only Child

I always liked the forest, thick
with life buzzing all around, vines that block
it all away—even the sun—keep you
hidden from it all.

                    Here I could be
alone, but never by myself.

It was always just Mama and me.
I was too young when my father died
to be left with a memory.
I had never lived in a hive
of family, sharing space with many.
When I was younger, I could play
        alone   for hours. I asked Mama once,
why didn't she go back
to her family, back to her village, on the top of the mountain.

She said, "There is a school here for you, Carlos,
in your father's village, and a road.
In Patrichál, the house of my family was crowded with
brothers, sister, uncles, cousins. Here we have something better.
Here we have   space."

Patrichál

Tía Rosa came to Chopán when I was eight.
Came to tell Mama their father
had died.
                    Tía Rosa stayed.   Mama
said it was time for us to climb the mountain.

She packed sacks
with blankets, food,
warmth.
                    And we walked.
For five days, we walked,
slept by the water and walked,
she named the plants we saw as we walked,
we sang and talked,   we walked and walked.

I can remember every step up
the mountain to Patrichál, but
I cannot remember
walking back down.

I Cannot Remember

There were plenty of berries to eat,
        fruit that was sweet.
I would not starve. Still,
I stopped to dig roots because
        I remembered Flora
showing me how.

It was after Roberto's brother was taken,
after his father was
gone. He was telling us his mother was
too sad to cook, asking Flora to make him
some soup.

She smiled at him with only her
eyes, took his hand, put it in the earth, pulled
up roots together,
showed us which roots were good to eat so we could make
our own dinners.

        I remember
the dirt Roberto threw at her, how she
                laughed and laughed.

        I cannot remember
which roots to eat or if she
                let go of his hand.

Smoke

I was walking
>   mind empty
>   eyes taking in all the

>   life

>   around me
>   mind empty
until

the wind carried it to me
>   like a message, filled my nose
>   with a taste of the

>   death

>   of a year's worth of planting and
>   I choked and
I breathed

the wind reminded me
>   would not let me forget
>   would not let me walk away

>   pulled me back

>   sent the memory with me
>   would not let me
leave it behind

Helicopters

The day we first heard them over our village,
like footsteps pounding on the sky,
we all looked up, pointed, waved. I wondered
what we must have looked like from that high.

They flew
over our village many times, searching the mountains for
something. We didn't care,
just reached our arms as high as we could, stretched
toward the sky, wanting
to be seen.

      We did not know to be
      afraid, did not know they were a storm
      of death, searching
      for a place to rain.

When I heard them in the woods alone, I
ducked, crouched
under a bush, made myself
small, tight, still, hidden.

Night

I stopped walking
before the night came so I would have
some light to find a tree, so I would have
my eyes closed tight before the dark arrived,
        cold dark.

Before I climbed, I took off the sweater,
  blue as the sky after a storm,
tied to my waist, put it on, trapped some heat
inside. I would need it for the night,
        cold night.

I wrapped my arms around the tree, fingers brushed
against my sleeves. My throat closed at the memory—
taking the sweater off the hook, stomping away from our house,
        warm house.

I wished I could go back,
let her touch my hair.

My Home

The walls were strong,
gray blocks of cement, that captured
all the warmth of the middle of the day, saved it
for the cool of night.

The floors were dirt,
packed firm and smooth,
earth, the same ground that had been there for days and years, holding up
so many dreams.

The roof was thick,
enough to keep out the rain that came each year and would not stop
for weeks and weeks.

I wondered
            if my house screamed
                        flames, spit
                                    smoke into the sky
            or

if it stood there
            alone
                        untouched
                                    and watched
                                                all the walls around it
                                                            burn.

I wondered
            if it stood there still.
                        Empty.   Cold.   Alone.

My Dream

sunset
in my village square in front of the church
I am tall
the size of a

man

Flora is there,
mashing up beans with a spoon,
slowly making them soft
then

standing up

on tiptoe, reaching her arm high above her head,
spooning a bite of beans into my
mouth, just the way a mother

would

feed a helpless baby

I squirm
I do not want her

help

they are laughing,
all the people of the

village

I cannot see them but
I can hear them

I want to

take

the spoon,
feed myself, but I
cannot,
my

arms

won't move

Flora does not seem to hear them
she looks at me
calm and patient
waiting like she knows what I am about to do but I
do not know
myself

I kick move fight thrash try to   *do*

              something

I woke up.
I could still hear them laughing.

Awake

The dream hung
over me with early morning mist,
left my face cool and damp,
clung to me, like the clouds
cling to the mountain.

I breathed in the wet
air, stretched my neck, let
the dream fade
b l u r r y   f u z z y

but the way
it made me feel — mad,
impatient, embarrassed —
lingered.

So did the laughter.

My skin prickled.
Alive.

I was not alone.
I could hear them:

soft laughter,
many footsteps,

trees breaking
in their path.

Someone coming.

Almost

| they came | faster | heart beat | faster |
| the sound | of them | got strong | then weak |

| *talking* | *footsteps* | *talking* | *footsteps* |

holdmybreath   closemyeyes

and then

sounds gone

| my heart | be gan | to | slow |
| I   knew | they had | moved on | |

I was still in my tree

Everything around me   had   shifted

What I Did

I did not follow them but
I walked swiftly, silently, in the place
where their sound faded.

I let my heart wonder
who they might be:
      people from my village
          coming to find me,
              maybe Roberto or
                  Tía Rosa with the baby or
                  Flora or

                        Mama

but my mind shook
my head. I knew
my heart was wrong.

    They were laughing. People
    from my village would not have been laughing.

I tried to swallow the rock that was in my throat because I knew
who would be laughing:

                  Soldiers.
                  The army.

A Shadow

I walked,
    a shadow on their path,
        stretching over sticks they'd cracked,
reached the edges of their talking,
           laughing,
              whistling.

Once I caught
    a glimpse,
        something moving up ahead: a gun
slung on a back of cloth stitched
           gray brown with green
             just like the trees.

I ducked, crouched
    low beside a bush, tucked
    my face into my sweater blue,
breathed in. Smelled home:
        warm, smoky—
          tortillas on the stove.

Breathing fast,   staying low   until their sound   faded away.

I stood up,   alone again,   realized I   was not the prey.

Later That Day

I got close
enough to hear
words, pieces of a language I did not know.
It was not the *lengua* of my village or
the words we learn in school: *español*.

They were heavy words,
like the fattest raindrops on top of our roof, beating
down fast and mad.
Until I heard
a smaller voice speak loud and clear in words I knew:

> *Estamos perdidos.*
> We are lost.

Lost

stupid soldiers
couldn't even

follow the
sounds

of a
river

up a
mountain

What I Realized

If they were lost, then
they searched.
      On the mountain,
      there is only
           up or down.
                They were going
                up.   Up is only
                    a village
                    much   smaller
                            than mine.

    Patrichál.
    Abuela.

Abuela

weaving mats on a stool by a fire in her house,

                                Abuela,

at the top of the mountain,

                                Abuela,

who rubbed my tired feet with herbs and I saw she,

                                Abuela,

had fingers just like Mama's,

                                Abuela,

         who was up there then,

             who did not know about those soldiers, lost
                 but on their way.

What I Did

I did not care about their

          guns,

or how their footsteps were so loud I knew
they were so

         many

or about the popping that I heard from the tree with the mushrooms or the
screams

that were so far away I could not tell whose
mouth had let them go or their

         guns,

or how small I was, how alone, or their

         guns,

    I just

         screamed

the loudest roar I could find inside, a roar
stolen from an angry jaguar, a roar that said
I am here, I am here, I am

         HERE!

Attack

I grabbed a limb and waved it in front of me
like it was on fire, and a rock,
a rock, was in my hand, and I
was raising back my arm and roaring
like a plane,
and letting go,
pushing that rock into the sky, as I saw a
head, the first head I saw, the rock
rushed through the air with my roar, landed
in a bush
in front of the one who
had pulled his gun
around, pointed it
right

at

me:

The boy.

The Rebels

A man
>>> stepped in front of me.
>>> I saw his back,
>>> heard his words:
>>>>> *"¡Baja el arma!"*
>>>>> *"¡Baja el arma!"*
>>>>> "Put down the gun!"

A woman
>>> stepped beside me,
>>> put her hand upon my arm,
>>> the one holding the stick,
>>>>> looked at me, spoke.
>>>>> I did not understand her words
>>>>> but her eyes said, "It's okay."

I stood,
limbs tight with tense,
while the backs in front of me moved,
>>> legs walking to him,
>>>>> hands patting his back,
>>>>>>> pushing down his gun.
>>>>>>> Words,
>>>>>>>>> lots of words
>>>>>>>>>>> I only heard:

>>>>>>>>>>>>> *sólo un niño.*

>>>>>>>>>>>>> "just a boy."

Eye to Eye

In front of me
I too saw
just a boy
pointing
a man's weapon.
The gun
shook
in his hand.
His body so tense,
it could snap
like a stick.
Eyes wide
and moving around
like water after a storm.
He gulped air like a hungry baby.
I stared him down and I saw
he was afraid.

He is afraid.
I stare him down and I see
he gulps air like a hungry baby.
Like water after a storm,
moving around,
eyes wide.
(Like a stick
could snap me!)
His body so tense
in her hand.
I shake
the gun,
a man's weapon,
pointing.
Just a boy
I see
in front of me.

Introductions

They talked, more words
I did not understand.
But then the man with a red cloth around his neck
put down his gun,
walked toward me with a smile.

"Buenas," he said. "You
are a surprise.
My name is Miguel."
                              He put his hand over his heart,
pointed to the woman
whose hand squeezed
my elbow still, "And this is Ana, the most
beautiful flower on any mountain."

She took away her hand, shook her head
from side to side, shot words
I did not know to Miguel,
who only sighed, but   they were both smiling.

"And that is
her brother, Hector," said Miguel with a nod.
I looked around and saw a man
scratching his arm. "He is here to keep her safe
from men like me." Miguel winked.
Hector shook his head.   They were still smiling.

Miguel pointed to the boy,
"This is their cousin Paco, who thought
you were an animal,
come to be his dinner this very night."
Miguel gave Paco a tap,
turned to me, lowered his voice to a whisper
that everyone could hear:

"Don't get too close to his mouth, *amigo,* because
he is very hungry, you see." Paco turned
red in the cheeks, but   even he was smiling.

I said nothing but   I felt my cheeks start to twitch.

The Rebels

Miguel said they were
        crossing the mountain,
        going to meet other rebels
        in a place called Ixchandé.

Miguel said they were
        moving in secret,
        hiding from the army,
        planning a way to keep the people safe.

Miguel asked
        what was my name,
        where was I going,   and
        where was I from.

I said
        "I am Carlos,
        going to Patrichál"   and

        nothing more.

Walked and Talked

I did not plan to join their group,
but found
I was soon walking with them,
walking beside
 the boy.

At first we were
silent until he said,
"*Lo siento.* Sorry
about the gun. I thought you were
 something wild
from the woods
coming to attack."

 I laughed
because there is nothing
in these trees that would attack with that much noise.

He grinned,
said, "But, *amigo,*
what was your plan with that stick?"

I shrugged, looked
away, felt my face get warm.

 "I thought you were the army."

Paco spat on the ground,
pinched up his eyes.

"*Nunca.* Never.
They came to our village one night,
looking for all the men they could find,
took away my uncle
 and others.

My aunt and my cousins went
from office to office, camp
to camp, asking
where the men were being
held.   But they got
no answers.

That is why
I am here now."
            He grabbed his gun.
"Fighting for
my people."

I nodded just a bit,
as my foot tripped   stumbled.
            I stopped walking,
bent down to see if a nut or seed or stick
was stuck inside my shoe.

There was nothing there.

Paco

Paco talked
a lot.

He told me all about his family:
  father and brother—older, picking fruit in California,
  sister—older, a baby of her own,
  three sisters—younger, always following him around,
  brother—small enough to stay wrapped up on the back of their
  mother,
  aunts, uncles, cousins, too,
  all live in the same place by the shore
  where they eat fish soup and the meat from crab and the ground
  is flat, so flat you can see people coming from far away before
  they land in his village.

After he talked and talked and
talked, he asked, "*¿Y tu familia?*"

I told him, "They live in Patrichál."
I looked up to the sky.

Permission

I walked beside him. We were
the same height, same size, same,
except he was not afraid
of the bullets on his chest,
except he knew what he was doing, except
he had a plan.

I asked Paco, "Your mama
let you be a rebel?"

> He cocked
> his head to the side, stuck out
> his elbow, thumped his hand against his chest:
> "I am the man
> of the house now,
> Carlos. I did not need
> to ask."

Flora

I remember a day in the cornfield,
        a day when I was supposed to be cleaning
            out the chicken pen,
        a day when I was hiding in the stalks instead
            with my friends.
When I heard Mama call my name, I sighed,
                  said good-bye,
                  heard Flora laugh,
    saw her cover her mouth with her hand,
    bend her eyes in sympathy
because there were too many
people in her mama's house to ever
call one home.

We Ate

We walked to the edge
of the trees, drank from the stream,
gathered limbs.

I built
the fire.

Miguel opened up the sack
he carried on his back, pulled out cans:
      beans in one,
        peaches in another,
stuck in his knife,
pulled out a peach,
plopped it into his mouth,
passed the can and a smile to me.

I took the can, ate a peach,
made a smile of my own.
My fingers stuck with sweet.

"We will sleep here tonight," said Miguel.

The fire warmed the front
of me, made me feel
    a chill   at my back.

Hector passed me a
cloth.   I unfolded the corners:

      tortillas.

"They are just a few
days old.   We got them
from a village down below."

The bag got heavy in my hand.
Paco watched me. I
picked up a tortilla from the top, put it between
my hands:
      cold,   tough,   rough,   old.

               A choke
               rose up in my throat,
               I tried to swallow it down.
               My eyes blurred
               the tortilla in my hand,
                  disappearing
               all its specks of
               brown.
                        I heard
               sounds of mouths
               chewing food,
               words,
                       closed my
               eyes,   rubbed the tortilla
               between my fingers until
               it crumbled:
                    dry,   old,   cold.

Chopán

I forced the air into my lungs,
asked Paco, "Where
were you coming
from? Where
have you been?"

He said, "A mission. We were
sent to San Fernando, where we hoped
to gather volunteers
to bring back to the camp to train."

"How many
did you get?" I asked.

Miguel answered for him, "There was no one left
to recruit. The day before we got there,
there was a massacre
in a nearby village. A village
we had been through
only a few days before.
Most of the people in San Fernando fled
when they heard the news."

My fingers tingled, my heart
got loud. "A massacre?"

Paco shook his head.
    Hector poked the fire.
        Ana sighed and frowned.
            Miguel said, "*Sí, amigo.*
            It was an awful
            thing to see. We went straight there
            after we heard the news."

"We were too late,"
Paco said. "Too late to kill
some soldiers."

        "Too late to help
        the people there at all,"
        Miguel agreed. "Everything had been
        burned. The houses —
          gone. The fields —
          destroyed. The people —
        only a large pile
        of dead bodies in a trench
        down by the lake.
        A mass grave. Very sad
        to see."

                No matter how much air I
                breathed, I could not
                fill my lungs.
                "Where?" I asked. "Where?
                What was the village
                name?"

Miguel looked
right at me.

"Chopán."

Ears

They talked

for minutes more, describing

what they saw.

The words   floated   all around me but

could not come through

my ears, clogged
with fuzziness   until

something
 pierced
 through:

"... the lady with the tortillas, I saw that yellow *tzut*

with the birds among the heads
in the pile..."

Sleep

Inside my head, something
  turned off,
    something went
        to sleep.

        I blinked.

        Watched myself
        dust off my hands, nod
        good night.

Miguel offered me his blanket,
insisted he would share with Ana
only for my sake —
        wink, wink.
His blanket looked soft, warm in the middle of others,
close to the fire,
low to the ground
where the smoke did not reach.

        But I stood,
        walked back into the jungle,
        climbed into a tree, to sleep
        from a spot where I could see.

Cloud

I climbed
my tree, nothing to see
after all.

We had reached
that point in the climb, that moment
on the mountain when
you are stuck
in the clouds.

I could not see
up. Could not see
down. I
could only see
what was right
in front of me.

Everything else
was covered in haze. Nothing
to do but wait
until I moved
out of it.   Up
                    or Down.

I Talked to God

I gripped the tree. Tried to make
a deal with God:

"If I turn around,
walk down,
I will find they are all alive."

Insects chirped, trees
whispered. God
said nothing.

"But some?" I asked.
"Someone will be there, someone
alive in that village.
Flora? Roberto?
Mama?"

God said nothing.

I squeezed the tree, felt
my throat clench.

"Did you see
what happened? Did you?
The trees saw. The earth
soaked up the blood, took in the pain. Did you
just turn away?"

Everyone

Everyone in Chopán went to church   sometimes
even Santiago Luc, who still
   counted the days in ancient ways,
   still traveled to the caves below the old
   temples, to make some smoke,
   sing to the gods, chant their names.

We were all sprinkled with holy water.
We were all given the name of a saint.
We were all taught to confess our sins,
give up some of what we have to God.

    I was not the only one.

We all knew the words to say, "*Dios te salve, María, llena eres de gracia.*
          Hail Mary, full of grace.*"

    I was not the only one.

Monkey

The next morning, Paco
woke me, standing
beneath my tree, shouting,
    "O o o o e e e e e oo oo.
    Come down, *monito*.
    Hector is boiling *café*."

I smelled the coffee
bubbling over the fire as I
climbed down the tree.
Paco brought his hands

up to his shoulders, crouched down
low to the ground,
made his monkey sounds.
Hector frowned,

shook his head at Paco.
Only Miguel saw I did not mind
being called a monkey.
He laughed,
        "Maybe *el Señor Mono* can
        teach us how to sleep in a tree.
        Might be better than this cold,
        wet ground."

    "*Sí, monito,*" Paco said. "You
    will have to teach us. We can't all be born
    knowing how like you."
    He gave my arm a gentle push.
    "Not all of us are monkeys."

Sleeping in Trees

Two weeks before the army left,

all the men in our village held a secret
meeting—decided everyone must
sleep that night in the forest.

Not everyone went.   Santiago Luc stayed,
wooden stool propped at the edge of the *maíz*, gripping his
cane,   guarding our corn,
keeping it safe,
from creatures of night.

Most of us went:
        babies on backs,
        children ran ahead,
            climbed up the side of the mountain,
            leaped into the arms of the forest,
                tucked themselves into beds inside bushes,
                pillows of moss, blankets of leaves.
                    A few men climbed up
                    high, into the trees,
                    keeping watch.

I found a place,
ground soft and cool   but I
could not sleep
on forest floor where things
crawl, creep, slither   without
warning.
        So when it was dark, I climbed
high into the branches, high
as other men, tucked myself
into the trunk, solid at my back,
where I could sleep.

Next morning, the sound
of people rustling in the plants
shook me   awake.
We all walked down the hill to the village,
where the tops of roofs seemed to look
up at us and say,
          "What are you doing up there?"

At the edge of the corn, Santiago Luc was still
there,   silver hair
resting on the curved top of his cane. He
opened his eyes, crinkled
his face, cleared his throat:

          "The corn is safe."

Morning

All morning, we walked.

Paco
> threw sticks at trees,
> talked and talked and talked and talked,
> aimed his gun into the sky until
Miguel
> > made him stop,
> > told some jokes,
> > whistled a tune,
> > asked for just one kiss from
> Ana
> > > shook her head,
> > > walked faster than us all, always in the lead,
> > > didn't say much but sent
> > > smiles to me and worried looks toward
> > Hector
> > > > walked in the back, always
> > > > last   glancing over his shoulder now and then
> > > > not saying much at all, nothing to

> > me.

Marching

I walked
beside them
all morning,
my footsteps
matched their
own,   just
like I
was marching
with them,
just like
I was
brave enough,
strong enough,
old enough
to fight
for my
village, fight
for my
home, fight
like a
man.

Not Afraid

Paco said he was not afraid
of the army.

He rested his hand
upon his gun,

said he could not wait
to feel the thrill
of watching some die.

He wanted to kill
one soldier for each
person in his village—gone.

He counted them, fingers shooting
up for each one he named:
       "Maria Gomez, just a teacher,
       she was the first, then they shot
       her brother, Jaime.

       "Mariano Choc is three," he said, holding up
       another finger. "They hung him from a tree."

Paco kept counting.
  I put my fingers
in my pocket, fit as many
marbles in my hand as I could,
  shot them

from my fingertips
to the bottom of my pocket
one at a time, counting.

       "Number nine was Padre Polanco—can you believe
       they would shoot a priest?"

Paco kept counting.
  I put my fingers
in my pocket, shooting
marbles, counting
    each shot
I made.
        "Then they met some men at the docks, took them
        away, nobody knows where.
        Gregorio, Ernesto, and Tío Julian—eleven, twelve, thirteen."
        He put his fingers down, dropped his
        hands to his sides,
        shrugged. "Thirteen is a lot of people
        disappeared
        from just one tiny village."

I squeezed the marbles, thought
about all the people squeezed
into the house with Flora, counted up her family,
my fingers in my pocket:
        Thirteen.

Thirteen people in her house
alone. How many
in all of Chopán?

An Invitation

Paco said, "You should join us,
monito. Come
with us to the camp."

I moved my hand
inside my pocket, wrapped my fingers
around the marbles.

"*Sí, sí,*" said Miguel. "You
have the look of a captain
in the making."

I said,
"I don't know."
Fingers on the marbles.

"Come on, *amigo.* We
can fight together."

"Paco signed up, I think,
just to get some good-bye kisses
from all the girls in his village."

Paco laughed, nodded, said, "Ah—
maybe that is the problem. Maybe
Carlos has a girl at home he cannot
bear to leave. What is her name, *monito?*
The prettiest girl in your village?"

I shook my head,
tried to clear away
my mind but
too late.   I saw the faces
before me,   faces of

Chopán.   I felt
my throat start to close
                stood up,   crawled
up on the rock behind me, big enough
for me to stand, tall
enough for me to see
          over the trees.

The View

From that high I saw
Xuba, the volcano —

used to be the thing
our village feared the most.

The Rock

I was sitting on the rock
above the heads and sounds
of my companions. I took
out the marbles, lined them up
in a groove
on the stone.
        Wondered
           how it would feel to hold
              a gun,
     aim it at
another man.

                  Wondered if
              I squeezed
           the trigger I
             could destroy
         the laughter I heard
      in my dreams,
        erase it   blow it   into many pieces
        never   have to hear the sound
               again.

I concentrated so hard on shutting
out the sound
that I did not hear
footsteps behind me.

Marbles

Paco scooped some up in his hands, shook them
side to side in his palms.
"I had marbles when I was
little," he said.

My heart pumped heat
into my cheeks.
"I just like the way they feel
in my pocket," I said.
"Smooth, slick, always cool."

Paco squeezed them in his fingers,
nodded his head at my words, then
grinned at me. "I'll shoot you
for them.   Winner gets keeps."

I shrugged.
Like it did not matter.

We played. Shot marbles
on the ground.
I watched Paco pinch
        his fingers around the shooter, pinch
        his eyes up every time, and when
I took the final piece,
        he shrugged his shoulders in defeat,
I shrugged mine too as if
it did not matter.

I slid them back
into my pocket with a secret
sigh, felt myself
unclench, let out a
breath I did not know
I held.

Guerilla

I imagined
    how I would look
    with bullets for a belt.
I wondered
    if Miguel
    would take them away
    when he found out I did
    nothing   to stop the army from taking Chopán.
I pictured
    myself arriving at the camp in Ixchandé,
    pictured myself shooting soldiers, taking
    revenge for all of Chopán.
I remembered
    Mama urging me to stay away,
    Santiago saying this was not our war.
I realized
    I had nowhere else to go.

In the Sky

Paco was telling me about this girl
in his village—Dominga—describing her with
words like flowers, with his hand upon his heart,
talking loud enough for everyone, everything
in the trees to hear, too loud
to have fear
or shame

when we heard

the helicopters

We Ducked

Miguel did not need to tell me
to find a bush,
make myself lower than the leaves,
tuck my face into my knees
and be
still.

We all took cover,
waited
still   quiet   until

the sound of spinning blades   faded.

My Sweater

Miguel's arm pulled me
out from branches thick
with thorns. He tugged
on the sweater around my waist.

> "*Monito,* your sweater
> is too handsome for these woods. Let me
> tuck it safe inside my pack until the night."

I moved my fingers to untie the knot of sleeves,
noticed my hands
  were shaking.   Miguel must have seen
this too but he said only,
> "You will need
> fatigues, clothes green as trees, if
> you stay with us."

I handed him my sweater,
slowed down my breaths.

Rebel Attire

"Your clothes," I said. "They are the same
as the army's."

> "Not quite," he said. "We have rubber boots—not leather.
> And our guns are not as fast.
> But Carlos—"

I saw a twinkle in his eye.

> "You can always
> tell the difference
> between the army and the rebels."

He moved his hand up to his hair,
weaved his fingers into curls.
> "We rebels have more hair,"
> he said, and winked.
> "And so we have more women."

Ana cleared her throat
behind me so I would turn to see her

                                        roll her eyes.

Stop for Lunch

Miguel decided we should
just rest there
for a bit.   My stomach felt sharp pricks
of too much
empty   space.
But Miguel's pack
had no more cans, the tortilla sack
was bare. "We will get some food
at the village up ahead," he said.

So we chewed on leaves,
ate some roots, busied our mouths
to fool our stomachs.   Only Paco complained:
"I am starving,
mucha! My pants are way too loose. This has to be the longest
I have gone without meat to chew."

Hector grunted.   Miguel
just laughed, "Paco, be glad you are too
young to have traveled with a crew
up the shore to work the land—
las fincas."

Paco shook his head, "You can't fool me,
Miguel. Raúl told me the rich farmer feeds his crews,
hires women to cook up
what the workers like."

Hector grunted again.
Miguel laughed even more, his shoulders
moving up and down,
up and down.   "*Sí,*
amigo. This is true—if
what you like is *frijoles.* Only beans
to eat—every day—no meat,

no fish, no tortillas to pack
a belly tight."

Paco said
nothing.   Just frowned.

Then Miguel pointed his finger
to me, "That
is why we fight, Carlos,
against the rich man
whose fathers' fathers took our land,
who gives us just
a handful of beans,   *centavos,*
for cutting sugarcane or picking cotton from the earth,
the cotton that is the grandchild of
our grandfather's seeds.

One day, *amigo,*
we *campesinos* will defeat
the men who hold us down,

take back our Guatemala."

I nodded like
I understood, but I was confused, thinking
of the richest man I knew,
Juan Choc Túc,
remembering
how the army had hated him, too.

Music

Miguel took out a *flauta,*
    small, smooth,
    the color of bone.
        He blew
          warm air into one end;
    it came out from the other end, light,
    cool,   like a whistle, sounded
           like flat rocks skipping
        on top of a lake, leaving
             little ripples behind.
         He did not play a song, just
      made his fingers dance
           over the top of each hole, fingers flapping
        up and down
      like the wings of a bird. It made
         the jungle air feel lighter,
      softer,   t h i n n e r.

I took a breath and felt
my chest grow.

Miguel saw my smile,
asked, "Do you make music, Carlos?"

    I shook my head
    from side to side, but found
    myself making music
    in my mind:
      the light, hollow sound
      of the marimba.

Roberto's Father

Roberto's father played the marimba.

He'd tuck his mallets under his arm, and we
would help him carry it,
big empty box of wood,
nothing inside but air. Until

He lined up with other men,
Stiff jackets in a row,
Necks gripped tight
With ties,
Heads down,
Arms stretched out to reach

the wooden keys,
their heads all bowed down
together.   A dance of concentration.

Sticks tapping lightly,
    clink
      clank
        clink
          tapping the music
       tink
     tank
    tink
Making the hearts of the whole village
    tink
      clank
        clink
          dance and sing with happiness.   Until

they took him

lined up with other men
stiff jackets in a row
necks gripped tight
heads down
arms stretched out to reach   the end.

The Marimba

It sat silent,
empty, behind the shed.
Roberto's mother asked him to

    "Bring it out.
     Dust it off.
     Please. Make it sing."

He told her, "No
heart in the village
feels like dancing."

Hector

Hector did not talk
much. And when he did, it was in his *lengua*,
one I did not understand.

Hector had not said anything
about me staying with their group,
training in Ixchandé. When Paco brought it up again,
urged me to fight, Miguel
hushed him with,
> "Paco, leave him be.
> Maybe this is not his war."

I saw Hector
grip his gun, point his
back a little straighter.

I did not understand
the words he spoke next, but
his face was stretched
red and tight.

> Miguel listened, then
> said, "*Cuidado,
> amigo.* That fire
> will burn your soul.
> When you open the door to hate, you will find
> it swallows you whole
> and there is no
> life left inside."

When Miguel was finished, he looked right
at me, his face
serious for just a flash. I noticed then
that his words were in Spanish and so I
could understand.

Walking

We were walking then so high
that my ears felt tightly stuffed.
Every now and then we heard
army blades
turning in the sky.

Once the sound was loud
enough, close enough,
to duck again.
    This time, I saw Paco
grab his gun, point
it up, get his finger ready.
    Miguel
pushed down Paco's arm,
lowered his gun, said,
    "Do not waste
your bullets,
shooting at the sky."

Helicopter Clouds

I remember
                        one day in the cornfield,
                        seeing the army fly
                        over our village,
                        up, alongside
                        the mountain,
                        hearing them move
                        like a storm cloud
                        over the trees,
                        raining down bullets
                        onto the leaves.

I remember

                        asking Santiago why
                        they would waste
                        their bullets, shoot
                        when they see
                        nothing.

He said,

                        "A man who throws
                        a thousand stones
                        into the lake is not
                        trying to hit
                        a fish, just
                        make all the fish
                        afraid   enough to
                        swim away."

Waiting

Even though they had their guns,
  their belts of pointed bullets,
my companions were not hunters.

Hector aimed for a bird in a tree, hoping,
  craving meat to eat, but his shot
only sent the bird away.

When Paco tried, his bullet
  bounced from the tree, caused
all of us to duck.

              I laughed.
  Paco grinned, offered up his gun
so I could be the one

bringing us a meal. I shook
  my head, told him there was a better way
to get some meat.

          Then I showed them
  how to gather twigs, use some vine,
make a trap, showed them which flowers smell

sweet enough to be perfect
  bait. Then I showed them how to
wait —

sit beneath the leaves,
  still as a trunk,
silent as roots,

waiting, watching,
  watching, waiting,
until something came along.

Something

I did not see it
creeping up to Hector, smelling
with its tongue.

"Culebra!" Paco said,
using the end of his rifle
to point at the ground in front of Hector's boot.

Hector did not make a move.

Miguel pulled out
his knife, bent his knees,
moved his arm.

"¡Esperate!" I said. "Stop!"

Miguel did not take his eyes off
the snake on the ground, but turned
his head to me.

I took three steps, leaned
my head in close, saw its tiny
stripes.   "It has no
venom, *mirá*, look. It will not
cause us harm."

I moved my hand — quick — to its neck,
grabbed it behind its head, swung
my hand back behind my shoulders, and let it
fly away.

> Miguel laughed.   Hector
> nodded.   Paco said,
> *"¡Púchica!* That was
> some throw!"

In the Trap

The rabbit was small, shivering,
brown, eyes wide with fear.

Hector snapped its neck, slit
its hide, put it on a stick.

Turned it around and around
over the fire while we all waited.

Paco said it was hard
to wait for a bite of juicy meat.

I thought so too, until I touched
the fur on the ground by Hector:

     soft   still warm

When I took a bite of flesh,
all I could taste was smoke.

Campfire

The sun disappeared
as Patrichál came into view.
We stopped to sleep
just down the mountain from the village.

With lips that tasted meat,
Paco was in a better mood, whistling
by the fire, asking Hector
to tell a story.
                    Hector shook his head.

Paco looked at me. "Tío Julian,
the father of Ana and Hector,
is the storyteller in our village. At night, after *fiestas,* people
go to his *sitio,* wait
to hear his stories."

                    "What kind of stories?" asked Miguel.

Paco said, "All kinds.
But mostly he would tell
the tales the old ones passed along."

                    Shadows from the flames
                    began to dance
                    on Hector's face.

Paco turned
to me. "Do you
have a person in your village who
tells the stories?"

                    I did not mean to speak, but
                    my mouth opened:
                    "Santiago."

"He is old?" Paco asked.

I nodded.

"Do you know
any of his tales?"

I had heard
many of his stories but what my tongue revealed was this:
"He believes
in *nahuales*.
Tells stories about boys
who see their spirit animal when
they become men."

"*Sí,*" said Paco.
"My *abuela* told me once there were
shape-shifters, black-magic people who
turned into animals at night, slipped
all over town in darkness."

"No, no," I said. "This
is different. These are spirits who
help us find our purpose,
protect us, travel with us, keep us safe."

"And they are animals?" Paco asked.

"Yes."

"Like a monkey?"

I only smiled.

"*Sí, sí, mucha,*" said Miguel.
"This is true you know. I have two.
One is a jaguar, smooth
and fast, and one
is a fox." He winked at Ana.

She laughed, wagged
her finger, and spoke.
"Yours is a rooster, fat,
proud, loud."

I smiled, closed my eyes and saw
Señor Pancho,
Flora's rooster,
how he strutted around the hens,
the boss of the whole pen.

I remember.

I Remember

I remember the sound
  of Santiago
  singing
        like the song came from his nose — deep
        no instruments making music, just his voice singing words,
        making my heart hum

I remember the feel
  of Mama's
  cheeks
        always smooth, slick   as a hill painted with mud
        always calm, cool   when I would run to her,
                                    my face hot with fear

I remember the taste
  of balloons
  when you blow them up before a festival:
        gritty, bitter, stuck
        on your tongue like you just licked a thousand spoons

I remember the smell
  of Flora's
  hair
    cold and warm, like a sunny breeze was captured on each strand
    like the tiny flowers her grandmother grew behind their house —
the ones you chewed to make your stomach calm

I remember
  the bush
  in front of the church
  where I could fit inside
        cool ground   no sound
        branches hiding   me from everyone, a way to disappear
                                      but still be   there

I remember

my village

the way the corners met, the places where puddles
gathered and houses cast shade and the paint on the wall of
my neighbor that was peeled off in the shape of an owl

There

I searched for a tree to climb to see
the village up ahead

at last
we were there

I felt some calm until
my heart fluttered its wings and I shook
away the thought that
tomorrow would be here soon

> Tomorrow Abuela would ask
> > where Mama was, how I
> > could leave her behind
> Tomorrow my new friends would know
> > how small I was
> Tomorrow I would need to choose
> > what to do   where to go
> Tomorrow
> > I might be brave
> > enough to be a soldier of the army of the people, brave
> > enough to stop running away

> tomorrow

I started to climb a tree but saw
it was taken by an owl,
who did not look my way, just
dove into the night, off to find
a meal

Woke Up in the Dark

I woke up
in my tree
with a   snap
        fast
like something had pinched me
        awake   I heard
nothing but in front of me I saw
        the owl
perched on the same branch as me
closer than we'd ever been

I knew I could reach out
     touch his feathers
       but I didn't
            I watched him
           watch me
              for a while then I
              closed my eyes
                smelled his scent
                 warm   soft   full
                  from a night
                   of hunting
                    I wondered
                 where he had
                 been, what
                  he had seen,
                 what
                 he had
              killed

     "Whoo!"

He called me
awake, pulled my eyes open,
stared into my face, calling,
like he was speaking right to
   me.   It made
my heart   thump   in my chest and
suddenly
            I was afraid.

He looked
at me, gave a hoot, dove
into the night.   I gripped
my tree, caught
my breath, strained my ears to hear.

           He was gone.

But far away
in the sky
I could hear thunder.

Not Thunder

helicopters

I Knew

They were coming
  there

     right there

     right then

"Wake up!" I yelled to the blankets by the trail of smoke,
"*¡Apúrense!* Quick! They are coming!"

I did not tell my body what to do   it just
moved
      down the tree
        up the ground
          through the cold wet gray
                    running
                      climbing
                        scurry
                        hurry   up
                            into the village
                                straight to the place
                                  my feet knew to go

Abuela

She was stooped
outside her hut, pushing
logs into a pile,
preparing to build a fire before
the sun arrived.

"They Are   Coming!   Now!   The   Army!   Quick!"

My words
were in a pant.

She raised
up her shoulders, dropped
her wood, moved her hands
up to her face.

"Carlos?"

"Get everyone
to the trees!"

I gulped
three more breaths

then

ran.

I Ran

       all over the village

I ran

       knocking on doors

I ran

       calling out a warning

I ran

       from one house to the next

I ran

       my arms spread wide like wings

I ran

       pushing and pecking them all in front of me

I ran

       moving all of Patrichál, every last one of them, into the trees

I flew

In the Woods

Every person in that tiny village stood
huddled in the woods,
waiting for

me.

I came in last, saw them standing in a huddle, unsure.

> "Scatter!" I said. "Don't
> bunch up. Climb a tree."

A woman lifted
her daughter onto a branch, climbed

up behind her.   A few other
people moved.   But most stayed

in a huddle,
arms empty,

eyes on me.

The People of Patrichál

I noticed then
they were small:
> grandmothers shrunken in,
> grandfathers bent on canes,
> children.

I scooped up a
boy, placed him on
a limb, said,

"Wrap your arms
around the trunk as tight
as you can. See if you can stand there
in that hug
without shaking
a single leaf."

Hurry

the sound of blades
slicing the sky

thud thud thud thud

was clear then

thud thud thud thud

near then   loud

thud thud thud thud

only a dozen or two
people to tuck
into trees

thud thud thud thud

there was a girl
my age

thud thud thud thud

helping

thud thud thud thud

with hair woven into an orange ribbon

when the ground
held no more
feet I
climbed

thud thud thud thud

into a tree
of my own and looked
up to the sky

thud thud thud thud

the trees were thick
there   I could not see

thud thud thud thud

helicopter blades but

thud thud thud thud

I could hear them loud

THUD THUD THUD THUD
THUD THUD THUD THUD

then

BOOM

like
something
crashed
inside
my
chest

my
ears

e x p l o d e d

the
trees
rang
swayed
but
stayed
put

Smoke

The sky
hissed
again and again

rain of death

dropped thuds to
the earth below

soon
the morning pink was smothered
up by gray
thick and strong:
          smoke

I Saw

    I put my eyes on the place where Patrichál   was

I saw black

I saw gray   smoke choking   everything

I saw flames   smoke moving fast   flying up
                    finding a way   to leave

I saw it all

I saw
I saw

    I did not look away
        even though the smoke came to my eyes   stung
I saw
I saw

I
  did
  not
  blink

Patrichál

tunnels of smoke thick and dark
shot from all over the village, like
a cornfield with no rows,
the smoke all came together in the sky,
spread wide, reached
me in my tree,
covered up the whole mountain,
smothered everything

Minutes Later

the thuds
　　　　stopped
the hisses
　　　　gone
the sound of blades
　　　　faded

I blinked my eyes
looked around
　　　　smoke thick
　　　　trees thick
I saw

no one

Sounds

a baby cried
  just then
  I heard
a mother   shuffle   whisper

I closed my eyes
let out a breath   let go
of the tree

The People of Patrichál

They were safe

all of them

feet back on the ground

they came together
from the trees, walked together,
and stood there together

looking at me
just like before

every head was there

Circles

I walked in circles
   from bush to bush
     looking for:
       guns
          arms
             a red bandanna
          arms
       guns
     looking for,
   from bush to bush
I walked in circles

until
I tripped
   fell
         something
on the ground

La Flauta

I bent
to put it in my hands

smooth as bone
unbroken, whole

from this low
on the ground I saw   the hole

Inside

Behind the tree,
     fallen years ago,
     the earth moved aside—a trench.   Inside

Hector
waved.   Ana
coughed.   Miguel
climbed out first.

Talking in Smoke

"You are okay?"
I asked.   He waved away smoke
                            from his face. "*Sí,*
                            amigo, you
                            woke us up just in time
                            to find a place to hide."

"But the bombs?"
                            "They aimed for the trail of smoke
                            our campfire left.
                            We ran so fast, we left
                            our blankets on the ground.
                            I'm sure the army thought
                            we were tucked asleep inside."

I smiled.   He chuckled then, slapped
                            me on the back.
                            "You saved us, Carlos,
                            with your screech from the trees.
                            Woke us from our dreams.
                            We ran toward your voice."

I looked at Ana,
watched her smile, saw
Hector wipe his face.
"And Paco?"
                            Miguel's smile
                            stopped.
                              "He was climbing up your tree. . . ."

Paco

"Paco!"

"Paco."   "¡Paco!"

"Paco?

¿Dónde estás?"

we scattered
into smoke
running
calling

"¿Paco?"

"Paco!"

"¡Paco!"

Flames

I saw flames
    from trees
flames
    from the village
flames
    through the smoke

I did not see
    Paco

In the Trees

I found
the people of Patrichál
standing together
still
in the same spot.

        No Paco.

                Miguel came up the other side.
        No Paco.

                He looked at them, said, "Have you seen
                a boy in fatigues — Paco?"

        No one moved. Abuela turned
        to me, spoke
        in *lengua*, "Tell this man
        we have done nothing
        wrong. Ask him please
        to leave our mountain, leave
        us with some peace."

I blinked.
Shook my head.
"No, Abuela. He is not
one of them. He did not
drop the bombs. He is not
a soldier,   just a rebel."

        She said, "They
        are one and the same."

Two Tongues

No one in Patrichál knew
the Spanish tongue so I
stood between the people of the mountain
and the guerilla rebels
and tried to build a bridge,
one word at a time.

Help

No person from the village
wanted to help
the rebels, dressed
for war, carrying guns,
but when I
asked for help to find a friend

a boy

everyone began to search.

Searching

The smoke was thinning then. It was clear
the village
was destroyed
but no one moved
to gather things burning up inside
instead everyone
searched bushes low for Paco.

Everyone   except me.

I Climbed a Tree

in out in
out in out in
out in out in out
in out in out in out in
out in *My breath was fast*
step pull step pull step pull step
pull step pull step pull step pull
step pull *I climbed a tree*

arms squeezed
tree swayed

eyes closed

I

opened my eyes,
looked around.

I Could See

Smoke wove
in and out of leaves.
I could see
searching people
dying fires
falling leaves.
A few birds circled, looking down in alarm.
The sun was out.
The birds would find
another place to land.

I saw one spread its wings, glide
through limbs above. It was wide
enough to be   the owl.
I watched him
seem to fly in place,
like he was waiting
for my eyes to find him there.
Then he
dove. Over to the right,
quickly almost out of sight,
and landed on a branch
higher than me.

Under that branch, over my head, stuck to the trunk,

I could see

Paco,

almost
disappeared.

Through the Trees

I moved
from branch to branch,
sweeping silently,
until I was there —
underneath him,

close enough to see
his hands, gripping the tree,
knuckles white,
skin stretched tight.

No Answer

"Paco!"

"*¿Paco?*"

"Where did you learn to climb so high?
Or did you maybe fly?"

"Paco?"

"Paco."

"Paco—look at me."

Underneath the Limb

"Paco, *escuchá*.
Listen to me now.
It is over. They are gone. No more
thunder in the sky. Listen.

"Paco, listen.
Everyone is safe. Everyone
got out.
Safe. In the trees
like you.

"Paco?"

He Spoke

"I ran. I hid.
I climbed a tree.
Frozen. Like a child."

Down

I looked up
at him for a moment, saw his arms
gripped tight, his eyes
closed.   I
took a deep breath.

"*Sí*," I said. "Yes.
Like a child you climbed, high
into this tree, to find a place safe
so you could live
to be a man. Yes,
like a child you hid, found
some leaves thick
enough to tuck yourself
away. Yes.   But.

Paco. Now you must
come down. One foot at a time.
Chin pointed straight ahead.
Because when you do that,
when you leave this tree,
when you put your feet back on the ground,
you will be   a man."

Climbing Down

Paco looked at me.

I told him
with my eyes
that I understood.

He nodded, took a breath,
and then
climbed down.

In Patrichál

Soon people saw us walking through
the trees and the news
that he was found spread.

Here he is!   *¡Aquí está!*   He is here!

We all walked together
to the village, smoking still.
The flames were finishing their meal,
looking tired and full.
Chickens pecked the ground, not afraid
to burn their beaks,
the woodpile by Abuela's kitchen
had been swallowed whole.

There was much
to do.

In Two Tongues

Abuela asked, right away,
"Carlos, what are you doing
here? Why are you with
these soldiers? Where
is your mother?"

I dropped
my chin, looked at my feet. Then
raised my eyes back up.
Gave her words in *lengua*. Then
gave the words again
to Miguel in *español*.

"The army came.
Came to Chopán.
Left nothing behind
except a boy,
a child, hiding in a tree, not yet
old enough, brave enough,
to bring them to a stop."

Abuela touched her fingers
to her lips, closed her eyes,
whispered prayers up to the skies.

Miguel clasped my shoulder,
said, "Carlos,
we are lucky to have found you,
lucky to have been helped
by such a man."

I looked behind
him at Paco,
who nodded, said,
"Thank you, Carlos. You saved
my life."

Time to Leave

Miguel said, "We must leave,
head down the other side. We are close
now to the camp. We must warn them
of the bombs."

Paco said, "But
the village?"

"They will be safer
when we are on our way."

Even though Abuela
could not understand their words, I saw
her gather up some corn and squash
from a pile behind her shed.

She pushed it at them, then
told them with her eyes
it was time for them to leave.

I looked around and saw
all eyes on me.

What I Saw Before Me

A man with a red bandanna, grand ideas, the face of one who's strong,
a woman, proud but kind,
her brother, ready and prepared,
their cousin, a man, choosing his own path.

A village
small, quiet,
where no one spoke the language
of war,
a village full of people,
full of work to be done.

The Voices I Heard

Mama: "Stay away from those soldiers, Carlos."

Mateo: "Carlos always does what he is told."

Mateo: "It is time to be a man."

Miguel: "They've left us no other choice, no other path but to stand up and fight."

Mateo: "A man would fight for his village. Keep it safe."

Santiago: "It is not our war."

Miguel: "The army has taken
away our land, scared
away our freedom, silenced
the voices of all those we love   forever."

But I could still hear voices.
They were not doused
with fire.

A person's voice cannot be buried
deep into the earth.
It will walk on forever, as long
as there are open ears.

What I Could Do

I could
>   show the children how to catch a rabbit,
>   guard a ball, dig up roots.

I could
>   take the words in *lengua,* of the old ones,
>   turn them into Spanish,
>   when people come.

I could
>   chop wood,
>   gather eggs,
>   feed the chickens.

And when the time comes,
I could
>   show them all
>   how to sleep in trees.

Good-bye

I gave Ana
a hug, sent Hector a nod,
shook Miguel's hand, then
reached into my pocket,
handed Paco my marbles,
looked him in the eye,
said, "Keep them safe."

He gripped
my hand, nodded
his head, said,
"Que te vaya bien."

Later That Night

After the fires had turned to smoke,
supplies had been moved,
things had been shifted,
I sat
in a circle with all of Patrichál, listening
to an old man chant
some prayers. The incense he burned
cleared out all other smells in my nose,
filled it with something
new. When he finished, we ate
together. Some people sang. A few children fell
asleep in their mothers' arms.

When one asked me
where I'd been,
how I got to Patrichál,
I was not sure what to say.
After a pause, my mouth began
to move on its own:

"Do you know
about *nahuales*?" I asked.
The children shook their heads. I saw the old man
with the prayers look over to me, nod.
"They are animals," I said. "Spirits who
follow us around,
show us what we're meant to do,
and keep us safe.
One day when you are older
you will see."

A small boy at my feet was digging
in the dirt. "Do you have one?" he asked.
"Is it a jaguar?"

I turned, looked to the trees,
now shadows in the dark.
"It is a secret," I said. "Something
we keep inside."

He gathered up his marbles, grabbed
onto my hand. I found myself
leaning down, putting my face
to his ear.

"But I can tell you this," I whispered near.

"I am safe."

Chopán, Guatemala, 2014

Names in Stone

"Papi, where is my abuela's name?"
she asks, one finger pointing down the list
carved into stone.

"You will find her,"
I say, watching her scan down
the list of names.
"We will find her,
today.   Finally."

I move my eyes
down the list. Each time
I see a name, I see a face,
hear a voice.

One hundred fifty-four names on this list. But my eyes are drawn
like magnets to some right away.

> *Santiago Luc,*
> *Mateo Andrés Xocol Uc,*
> *Roberto Manuel Quíc Martín,*
> The name of my *tía Rosa* has a dash
> to the side with an added *infant child,*
> and I wonder once again what name
> my cousin had.

Today is
the day.
After days and years spent arguing
in courts, today we watch
men peel away
the soil, dig into the earth,
carry up the secrets
that were buried years ago.

Today, Chopán gets its turn
to speak.

It has been a town of ghosts
for far too many years.
Today, those of us who lived
here return.

I was not the only one.
Not the only person to survive.
Some were away that day, working
at the coast, or selling squash at the market in San Fernando.
Others ran.
Like me, they ran.
Fled to the trees. Hid
in bushes, found a way
to stay alive.

Today our roots
pull us back so we can make things
right for those we loved.

"Aquí!" she says. "I see it.
María Catalina Ramón Có."

"*Sí, mija.*
A lovely name it is."

"That's why you
gave it to me to share?"

I nod, even though her face has turned
back to the stone, her lips continue
sounding out the names.

Just then I feel
a hand upon my shoulder,
turn around to see
a woman, smiling up at me.

"Carlos?" She puts her hand upon her cheek, sweeps
her eyes over my face,
and laughs out loud.
"You are younger in my head—just a boy."

She laughs a quiet laugh
and gives a sigh. "I am sure
you do not remember
who I am."

I bend my face down close
to hers, take a breath
full of surprise. "Flora?"
I say, squeezing
my daughter's hand.

The woman laughs again.

I smile.

"I remember."

Glossary

abuela (ah-BWEH-lah): grandmother

Ah Xochil (AH SHO-cheel): an ancient Mayan name for a person with the eyes or face of an owl

amigo (ah-MEE-goh): friend

¡Apúrense! (ah-POO-rehn-seh): Hurry up!

aquí (ah-KEE): here

¡Aquí está! (ah-KEE ehs-TAH): He's here!

¡Baja el arma! (BAH-hah EHL AHR-mah): Put down the gun!

buenas (BWEH-nahs): short for *buenas tardes* (good afternoon) or *buenas noches* (good evening); it's how people in Guatemala sometimes say "Hello" to one another

café (kah-FEH): coffee

caminar (cah-mee-NAR): to walk

campesinos (cahm-peh-SEE-nohs): farmers, peasants, or poorer people who live in a rural setting

centavo (sehn-TAH-voh): Guatemalan coin, worth one one-hundredth of a *quetzal*

cinco minutos más (SEEN-koh mee-NOO-tohs mahs): five more minutes

cohetes (koh-EH-tehs): fireworks

cuidado, amigo (kwee-DAH-doh ah-MEE-goh): careful, friend

culebra (koo-LEH-brah): snake

Dios mío (dee-OHS MEE-oh): my God

Dios te salve, María, llena eres de gracia (dee-OHS TEH SAHL-veh, mah-REE-ah, YEH-nah EH-rehs DEH GRAH-see-ah): Hail Mary, full of grace (the beginning of a prayer)

¿Dónde andabas? (DOHN-deh ahn-DAH-bas): Where have you been?

¿Dónde están? (DOHN-deh ehs-TAHN): Where are they?

¿Dónde estás? (DOHN-deh ehs-TAHS): Where are you?

el Señor Mono (ehl SEHN-yohr MOH-noh): Mister Monkey

el tecolote (EHL teh-coh-LOH-teh): the owl

el tío de (EHL TEE-oh-deh): the uncle of

escuchá (ehs-koo-CHAH): listen

español (ehs-pahn-YOHL): Spanish

esperate (ehs-peh-RAH-teh): wait

estamos perdidos (ehs-TAH-mohs pehr-DEE-dohs): we are lost

fiestas (fee-EHS-tahs): festivals or celebrations

flauta (FLAW-tah): flute

frijoles (free-HOH-lehs): beans

las fincas (LAHS FEEN-kahs): the farms

lengua (LEHN-gwah): language

lo siento (LOH see-EHN-toh): I'm sorry

maíz (mah-EES): corn

marimba (mah-REEM-bah): a large wooden instrument, resembling a xylophone

*mariposas (*mah-ree-POH-sahs): butterflies

¡Mi Manuel! (MEE mahn-WEHL): My Manuel (a name)

mija (MEE-hah): my daughter (it's short for *mi hija*)

mijo (MEE-hoh): my son (it's short for *mi hijo*)

mirá (mee-RAH): look

mis compañeros (MEES kohm-pahn-YEH-rohs): my companions

monito (moh-NEE-toh): little monkey

nahuales (nah-WAH-lehs): animal spirit protectors

nunca (NOON-kah): never

Padre Polanco (PAHD-reh poh-LAHN-koh): Father Polanco (a priest's name in this story)

para que escarmienten (PAH-rah KEH ehs-cahr-mee-EHN-tehn): so that they will learn their lesson

pobrecito (poh-breh-SEE-toh): poor little thing

¡Púchica! (POO-chee-kah): an expression of amazement in Guatemalan Spanish. It's like saying "Wow!" or "You're kidding!"

qué bonita (KEH boh-NEE-tah): how pretty

Que te vaya bien (KEH TEH VAH-yah bee-EHN): a form of good-bye meaning "May it go well with you."

quetzales (keht-SAH-lehs): the Guatemalan system of currency/money

se durmió (SEH door-mee-OH): it (or he or she) fell asleep

Señor Pancho (sehn-YOHR PAHN-choh): Mister Pancho (the name of a rooster in this story)

sí, mucha (SEE moo-CHAH): yes, friends; an expression used among friends, short for *muchachos*

sitio (SEE-tee-oh): a site or place or room. In this story it's used like "his place," meaning his house.

sólo un niño (SOH-loh OON NEEN-yoh): just a boy

sopa de hongos (SOH-pah DEH OHN-gohs): mushroom soup

tía (TEE-ah): aunt

tienda (tee-EHN-dah): a corner store, almost like a little convenience store

tío (TEE-oh): uncle

tzut (SOO-teh): an embroidered cloth worn on top of the head

vení aquí (veh-NEE ah-KEE): come here

¿Y tu familia? (EE TOO fah-MEE-lee-ah): And your family?

Q & A with the Author

Is *Caminar* a real story?
Caminar is fiction. That means I made it up. Chopán is not a real place, and Carlos is not a real kid, but what happened to him and what happened to his village did really happen in Guatemala not too long ago.

Why were the soldiers and the guerillas fighting?
Oh, that's a tough question to answer. It's always hard to understand why people are fighting, especially because each side usually has their own ideas about what the argument is about. I think that the Guatemalan army felt they were fighting to stamp out communism, and to maintain control. The guerillas were fighting because they didn't like the way the government was treating them. In the midst of all that, there were many people who weren't technically on either side but caught in the middle and often killed.

What happened to all those people?
Many died. Still others were "disappeared," or taken by the army and never heard from again. Others left their village and moved to the city. Many left Guatemala altogether, leaving behind everything they owned, their way of life, their families and friends, and fled to Mexico or the United States, where they felt safer.

I thought people spoke Spanish in Guatemala. Why does Carlos speak a different language from Hector?
Spanish became the official language of Guatemala almost five hundred years ago, when the Spaniards came from Europe to the land we now call Guatemala. But for hundreds of years before that, there were many different languages spoken in Guatemala, such as K'iche, Kaqchikel, and Mam. Today, we call them indigenous languages. Many people in Guatemala, especially outside of the cities, speak them still.

Are you from Guatemala?
No, I'm from the United States, but I've visited Guatemala many times, and I lived there for five months while I was revising this novel.

Do you speak Spanish?
A little. But for this book, I had help from my husband, who teaches Spanish to college students, and from my Guatemalan friends.

Why did you write this story?
For more than ten years I've been really interested in Guatemala and saddened by what happened there a few decades ago. I've read many books on the subject and met many people who lived through the violence. The more I learned about what happened there, the more I felt that my country, the United States, shares a good part of the blame. It made me sad to realize that, and made me feel like I wanted to do something about it. One thing I can do is to make sure people know about what happened there, so that we can all find ways to help.

If you'd like to donate money to help people like Carlos find out what happened to their loved ones, you can check out organizations such as the Guatemalan Forensic Anthropology Foundation at www.fafg.org.

Acknowledgments

I wrote this novel while I was a student at Vermont College of Fine Arts, where I learned everything I needed to learn about being a writer. Many thanks to Shelley Tanaka, who listened to me explain my idea for a story and told me to hang up the phone right then and get started on it. And to Sharon Darrow and Julie Larios, two amazing poets and teachers, who helped me to craft poems that captured what I wanted to say, and to weave them into a book that told Carlos's story.

Big thanks to Kristin Sandoval for reading draft after draft of this story and offering up lots of good advice.

I am indebted to Marta Lidia Jimenez for aiding me in the cultural and linguistic nuances of this book and to Olga Reiche for reading the manuscript and helping me to maintain its authenticity and accuracy. Thanks also to Jarrod Brown and Erin Hagar for their help with the Spanish glossary. Any mistakes in this book are my own.

The Society of Children's Book Writers and Illustrators was kind enough to award me a grant that made my travel for this book's revision possible. I am very grateful for that.

I am fortunate enough to have a terrific agent, Tina Wexler, and two wonderful editors, Liz Bicknell and Carter Hasegawa, who all cared just as much as I did about Carlos and his village and about getting this story *right*.

Finally, to Jarrod, Gustavo, Isaac, and Luís, thank you for every "What part did you write today?" that you asked over dinner. I feel lucky to have a family that cares about stories just as much as I do.